The Song of the Distant Root

The Song of the Distant Root

by
Elizabeth Subercaseaux

translation and foreword by
John J. Hassett

Latin American Literary Review Press
Series: Discoveries
2001

The Latin American Literary Review Press publishes Latin American creative writing under the series title Discoveries, and critical works under the series title Explorations.

Library of Congress Cataloging-in-Publication Data:

Subercaseaux, Elizabeth.
   {Canto de la raiz lejana. English]
The song of the distant root / by Elizabeth Subercaseaux;
   translated by John J. Hassett.
      p. cm. -- (Series Discoveries)
   ISBN 1-891270-11-7 (alk. paper)
   I. Hassett, John J. II. Title. III. Discoveries.

PQ8098.29.U25 C3613 2001
863.64--dc21

                                                              00-056327

Cover Design by Juan Subercaseaux

Latin American Literary Review Press
121 Edgewood Avenue
Pittsburgh, PA 15218

NATIONAL
ENDOWMENT
FOR THE ARTS

Acknowledgments

This project is supported in part
by grants from the
National Endowment for the Arts in Washington, D.C.,
a federal agency,
and the
Commonwealth of Pennsylvania
Council on the Arts.

PENNSYLVANIA
COUNCIL
ON THE

ARTS

*This novel is dedicated to
Doris and Jim Vermeychuk*

Introduction

Born in 1945, Elizabeth Subercaseaux is part of what she has frequently called the first generation of Chilean women to put an end to her country's long tradition of relegating their role to the home and the kitchen. When she speaks of the women of her generation as survivors she alludes to the fact that they had to balance two roles: that of housewife and office professional. Many of her peers found journalism to be an attractive outlet for their talents and their commitment to social change. And it was particularly during the seventies and eighties of the Pinochet regime that journalists such as Raquel Correa, Patricia Verdugo, Delia Vergara, Malú Sierra, and Subercaseaux played an important role in bringing to the attention of the Chilean public the human rights violations committed by the regime and in mobilizing public opinion toward an eventual rejection of the dictator in the national plebescite that was held in 1988.

Subercaseaux's journalistic career began in 1975 with her founding of *El Peque*, a magazine for children. Later she wrote for *Cosas* and then *Apsi*, one of the principal publications of the political opposition during the harshest years of the dictatorship. Today she is a regular contributor to *Vanidades Continental* (Miami), *Caras* (Chile) and *Sábado* (*El Mercurio*, Chile). On a less frequent basis her articles also continue to appear in *Cuadernos Cervantes* (Madrid). Her early journalistic endeavors have produced three important books dealing with Chile's military regime: "Del lado de acá (Seen from this Side, 1982), "Los generales de regimen" (The Generals of the Regime,1983), and with Raquel Correa, "Ego Sum Pinochet" (1989), an extended series of interviews with the General which became an instant best-seller in her native country. In addition to these publications of a more journalistic nature, she is also an accomplished short story writer and novelist and joins an impressive group of Chilean women writers whose careers blossomed in the eighties and nineties that includes Isabel Allende, Diamela Eltit, Ana María del Río, Pía Barros and Marcela Serrano. Subercaseaux's literary career began officially in 1986 with the publication of "Silendra", a nouvelle, followed in 1988 by her novel "El canto de la raiz lejana" (The Song of the Distant Root). Since May of 1990 she has lived in the United States, and the intervening years have been ones of intense literary and journalistic activity. During this period she has published four novels: "El general azul" (The Blue General, 1992), "Matrimonio a la chilena" (Marriage Chilean Style, 1997), "Una semana de octubre" (A Week in October, 1999), and "La rebelión de las nanas" (The Rebellion of the Nannies, 2000).

The first of these explores a theme common in Latin American letters, the figure of the dictator and the exercise of absolute power, while the second parodies Chile's idiosyncratic approach to matrimony in the absence of legalized divorce."A Week in October" is the story of a woman who, faced with imminent death and a marriage devoid of passion, seeks refuge in a shortlived affair that perhaps may have been a creation of her own imagination and need to be loved. In "The Rebellion of the Nannies" Subercaseaux has written a highly political novel that explores the values of a society still tethered to the vestiges of its former dictatorship and its own exaggerated class consciousness as it enters a new millennium.

Subercaseaux's journalistic activity also constitutes a series of humorous yet profound reflections on the problems confronted by women as they make their way through a male-dominated landscape. These widely read accounts include "La comezon de ser mujer" (The Yearning to Be a Woman, 1994), "Las diez cosas que una mujer en Chile no debe hacer jamás" (The Ten Things a Woman in Chile Should Never Do, 1995), and "Eva en el mundo de los jaguares" (Eve in the World of the Jaguars, 1998). In 1998 she also published Gabriel Valdés: Señales de historia (Gabriel Valdés: Signs From History), an historical memoir of one of Chile's leading political figures filtered through the entertaining and flowing prose of Subercaseaux's journalistic pen.

Elizabeth Subecaseaux spent her formative years near Cauquenes, Chile at her grandparents' hacienda-style home called Santa Clara. For her and her siblings it was a magical place of unlimited spaces and horizons with some new discovery to be made around every corner they explored. Far from the hustle and bustle of Santiago, Chile's capital city, she found herself surrounded by the endless sea of her grandfather's vineyards, the warmth of the workers and their families, the sounds of barnyard animals, the smell of eucalyptus leaves as the wind rustled through the treetops, and the echoes of a nearby stream as it wended its way through Santa Clara's terraced hills. Today there is very little left of the Santa Clara of her youth. Gone are the vineyards. The land, expropriated by President Eduardo Frei's government in the mid-sixties under his administration's agrarian reform program, is now a sea of pine trees whose toxicity has gradually eroded the fertility of the once productive soil. Left standing is the large family house inhabited now by only the ghosts of the past. It is this past, this space preserved in memory that Subercaseaux frequently resurrects to different degrees in her narrative, but principally in "Silendra" and "El canto de la raiz lejana" (The Song of the Distant Root).

The Song of the Distant Root recounts Salustio's yearning for a place where a sense of solidarity and community prevails, unlike the locale in which he and his family live enveloped by solitude and the overwhelming presence of death. One night he dreams of such a place, called Tapihue, a village filled with the sounds and laughter of neighbors and their children. On the following day he sets out to find Tapihue in the hope of establishing a new community in which human beings might interact outside the confines of a devastating past. While his wife Clarisa perceives his efforts as nothing more that a misguided obsession that can end only in death, Salustio believes that Tapihue represents a genuine possibility to create a reality based on human warmth. In the pages that follow Tapihue emerges and as time passes it is populated by others who, like Salustio, seek an alternative to their solitary lives. Some of its most important residents include a priest, Francisco, who blesses himself backwards, says Mass from the back of the church reciting prayers that no one has ever heard before; a dentist called Esmeraldo but who also goes by the name of Rómulo and sometimes Juvenal; and Fulgencio, an ox that flies.

Whether Salustio invents such a place, called Tapihue, or actually founds it is never completely clear to the reader who, like the characters, must navigate through a world where myth, dreams and dementia all coexist. Tapihue is a corner of the world embodied by its geographical isolation and the indifference of the modern world's centers of power and influence. While a first reading of the novel does not clarify all that is contained within its extremely elliptical pages, the implications regarding the brutality of military dictatorship become more and more apparent, particularly to the reader acquainted with events in Chile during the Pinochet regime. Tapihue's landscape, rather than externally viewed, is captured from within the interior of its inhabitants. It is this ability on the part of Subercaseaux to construct her story from within that makes her narrative world so suggestive, so powerful, and at the same time so ambiguous.

Similarly, it is impossible to speak of this text without alluding to the lyrical quality of its language, a language that is reminiscent of the great Mexican writer Juan Rulfo. Subercaseaux's narrative, like Rulfo's, is filled with absences and the reader, much like the characters, must go in search of meaning in a world whose language flutters between the real and the hallucinatory. Here time has no definite chronological signposts: hours, days, months, years all come together in a kind of mythic continuum. However, as is typical of Subercaseaux's narrative, death is everywhere and no one escapes its insatiable grasp. Her prose is extremely lean and presents a narrative world that contains a minimum of external description of characters, events and surroundings. The author's talent lies in her ability to suggest rather than describe, to arrive at the essence of the fictional world through descriptive detail. She leaves the reader to fill in the gaps of the narration, and despite the lack of realistic description, we come away with a powerful and unforgettable image of Tapihue and its people.

Unlike the majority of her generational peers, Subercaseaux has chosen a rural setting as her source of inspiration but shows little or no interest in questions of local color or linguistic regionalisms. Instead, she opts for a mode of expression that is highly poetic and fragmented in nature which explores the certainties of a reality governed by the rational only to reduce them to the category of the elusive and the relative. And like Rulfo's Comala, Tapihue is a narrative space in which the past speaks more eloquently than the present, where the line between living and dead is not always clearly discernible, where anguish and guilt devour the moment, and where the search for personal identity and collective solidarity sets in motion an endless journey toward silence and death. In this process resides the fundamental difference between journalism and literary narrative for Subercaseaux. For her a journalist is nothing more than a transparent siphon through which information passes. But in fiction, she points out, the same reality can be reinvented over and over again and in each recreation it is what is suggested, what is not said, that demands the reader's utmost attention and creativity.

John J. Hassett

$\mathcal{H}$e came from the mountain. Almost three days and three nights of travel. He was tired. His godmother always used to say that when you walk without knowing where you are going the road you travel on is never one but two.

He had left Clarisa filled with bad omens, convinced that death was going to carry him off. Before departing he noticed she looked frightened and pale. She spoke about his obsession but that is not what it was about. It was the solitude of those mountains that always looked the same. It was the wind that suddenly rose up. The calm that appeared without warning. It was the language between the sky and the pines. It was the desire he had to live in a village with children, with balls bouncing through the streets, with neighbors' chickens walking around his yard.

"A village doesn't sprout just like that, Salustio. Things have to exist first and then later people come. It's true that these mountains infect you with their sadness but all villages emerge from history. They're in books from the very beginning. There has to be a priest to hear your confession and to say Mass on Sundays. There have to be streets. Don't be stubborn, Salustio. You've become obsessed. And, besides, you're going to meet up with death. Vitoco says that she's always waiting, ready to carry travelers off with her. He says that her face is black and that she has holes for eyes. That she has no eyes, no hands. That she has two stumps and she hurls herself upon men and envelops them in her cold and heavy breath. She wraps them up in her entrails. Forever. Because Death never gives them back…"

Salustio listened to her in silence.

One night he dreamed a village. It had houses and a church. There were children playing with two sticks. There was a priest with long bones and infinite eyes looking toward the tops of the pine trees. Salustio was sitting in front of his house and the neighbors' hens and ducks were walking through the yard. When he saw the name Tapihue written on a board his whole body began to tremble. On the following day he decided to set out.

"I'm going to look for that place," he said and left.

Clarisa watched him go with her eyes fixed on him; José waved goodbye to him and the two stood in the doorway until Salustio was lost from sight.

"Death is going to find him," she said as she swallowed a tear.

The water from the stream called La Toribia ran almost without sound. Everything else was surrounded by silence. The tops of the pines moved a little. The myrtle bushes, quiet and glittering, were loaded with fruit.

There were two old *quillayes* and a cluster of oak trees with *quintrales* covered with *digueñes*.

"This is the spot," said Salustio and he sat down on the ground. He felt free of a fatigue that had entered his body some time ago. Light and unburdened, that's how he felt, and when he thought about the mountain he thought about it in another way, as if something had died and he were saying the final words.

"There have to be Sundays. So you don't have to work. So that the week comes to an end. So that time is not a straight line, formed by days that arrive nameless and depart leaving nothing behind; and by nights that pass without anyone remembering them. You can't live without Monday night, without Thursday afternoon, without Tuesday morning. You can't live without remembering such and such happened on Saturday and that it was Sunday when the sky closed in upon itself. It's impossible to live knowing that time passes but without understanding how it passed." Then he thought that the mountain was too solitary. There was nothing. Just the mountain and the quiet. It's true that Vitoco and Enedina were there and their children who never spoke, but they lived far from his house. He hardly ever saw them, and Salustio was afraid of children. When he recalled the one with the greenest eyes, Martín, he started to pray the Our Father but he could not continue. He had forgotten the words and the *Alabado*, he could sing only half of it. "I no longer remember how to make the sign of the cross," he thought. At that moment a *queltehue* flew down. For just an instant the eyes of Salustio and the bird met. Salustio listened as the bird spoke to him and then he thought about Clarisa. "She's walking around the house like a dead woman with José holding on to her tightly. As if they were one. I want to sleep with her and have the child sleep in another bed."

He met her one day while she was chasing a speckled hen. That same afternoon he saw her at the grape harvest in Santa Clara. She left her basket on the ground, looked at him, smiled a little and started running through the bushes. Salustio chased her and when he caught up with her they rolled on the ground. Salustio sensed his whole body harden and Clarisa felt a warm sensation.

Nightfall found them naked.

They were married in the church of Santa Clara and the reception was held at Melania's house. The bride and the groom danced the *calladito* and the *corrido* entitled "What sorrow the soul feels." One song happy, the other sad. "Just to make sure the owls that brought bad luck were all dead," Melania said. They ate lamb and *chanchos en piedra* and drank wine from the cooperative. When all the guests had gone, Salustio hugged Melania, shook Ramón Hernández's hand and left with Clarisa. Melania swept the floor and turned off the victrola. That night the wind started to blow and Melania wept a little.

That same day Salustio and Clarisa set out for the mountain. There they built their house. The coal business did not pay much but they could survive.

When he returned home and told Clarisa that he was still alive, that death had not carried him off, that he had found the right place for Tapihue, that a *queltehue* had spoken to him, his wife looked at him with a sad expression on her face and in the deepest part of her eyes a light went out. Salustio didn't realize this and he spoke to her about how the pine trees moved, about the water of the silent stream. He told her that in the hollow there were myrtle trees and oaks with *quintrales* filled with *digueñes*.

"Let's go live in a village. Let's leave behind the sadness of this mountain that is beginning to stamp itself upon our faces, leaving our eyes looking like those of a madman. Making them rounder, emptier and staring into space…What's wrong?"

"You've gone crazy. *Queltehues* don't speak. In that hollow we're going to be just as lonely as we are here. Why don't we go live in a village that already exists?"

"Tapihue will be our village. We'll have a priest to hear confessions and say Mass on Sundays. We'll have a cemetery to bury our dead. The *queltehue* told me."

"You're nuts, Salustio. You've got the same sickness that killed Ramiro Hernández. Death didn't devour you but craziness certainly has," Clarisa said, almost shouting, but Salustio was already counting the adobe bricks.

"And José? Where are we going to leave him while we build our house?"

"At Enedina's."

"They don't even have enough to feed themselves."

"We'll take them a sack of wheat."

"José doesn't eat wheat."

"We'll give them the hen."

Salustio kept counting the adobe bricks, and then the beams needed for the roof, and next he walked off the size of the room, and finally he sketched it all on a piece of paper.

"And the people? Where do you think the people will come from?"

"They're already on the roads looking for a place. Some in wagons. Others on foot. Priests, women and children. Even hens that have been abandoned along the way," he answered as if he were asleep and, for the rest of the afternoon, he didn't say a word.

Salustio was, at times, a quiet and happy man. He remembered the day when someone left him among the grape vines of Santa Clara. He had a piece of paper in his hand. "Salustio" was written on it. He must have been about four years old and the leaves of the grape vines hid him from sight. Melania was the one who found him. When she asked him his name he held out the piece of paper and did not answer any of her other questions.

"An abandoned child!" Melania shouted and the campesinos came quickly. She raised him and Ramiro Hernández, her husband, crazy since birth, did not realize there was another child in their home.

Up until the time he married Clarisa he lived in Santa Clara, the land of a señora who spoke with the dead and flew from room to room. They said she had sky blue eyes and white hair. That she wore trousers and a blue wool cape and she spoke with a foreign accent. That she was transparent, they said, but Salustio never saw her.

That night he spoke in his sleep and Clarisa heard a different voice coming from him. She became frightened and shook him.

"What's wrong?" he asked, rubbing sleep from his eyes.

"A strange voice was coming from you. A voice like that of a prophet. You're not sick, are you?"

"No, nothing's wrong with me."

"But that wasn't your voice."

"Sometimes strange things happen. The *queltehue* said bad times were coming."

Clarisa drew the blanket around her and before falling asleep murmured:

"You spoke about an empty field with bright stars all around and you said that there was an old man sitting on a mound of earth. But that wasn't your voice."

On the following day they left for Enedina's house. They took the sack of wheat and the hen with them. And José's blanket. They made their way in silence that was heightened by the silence of the mountains and the sky, and in the midst of all of this quiet a cloud enveloped them and the wagon took off in flight. It did not take them long to get there.

Enedina said she would take care of José as if he were her own child. Actually she did not say this because she never said anything, but she did hug him. Vitoco laughed at the non-existent village and said that later they too would move.

"When there's a priest," he said.

The children said nothing. Salustio looked at them somewhat angrily, but they did not care or maybe they did not realize how he was looking at them.

They made the journey back in even greater silence. It took them half a day.

Salustio said that they would leave as soon as possible and that same afternoon they loaded up the wagon.

They put the pig and the one hen they still had in the wagon. The rooster took off and Salustio had no desire to go looking for him.

"It's not worth the trouble," he said. He's old and he's going to die anyway."

The wagon came to a stop and Salustio pointed to the hollow.

"There it is," he said..

Clarisa washed her face in the stream. Then she sat down beneath the oak trees and continued looking at the sky.

"Here's where we're going to build our house," Salustio said, pointing to the myrtle bushes. "The myrtle bushes will be part of the yard. Do you like this place?" he asked her, but she was already some place else.

She worked like those women who were not there when you spoke to them. Salustio did not mind that a woman who seemed to be asleep was helping him. Melania had told him that when the absence takes control and people start walking like the dead who say nothing, there is no reason for alarm, because just as quickly as the absence comes it also goes away.

One morning Clarisa opened her eyes and spoke. "Tapihue...I like the name of this village that isn't a village," she said. Then she washed her face and started to work. She chased the pig away and made herself a broom, swept the house while singing the *Alabado* and laughed as she ran after the hen. Salustio watched her out of the corner of his eye and she did not notice when he tried to make the sign of the cross.

A few days later Vitoco and Enedina arrived. They came to drop off José. Vitoco said that in three more months they too would move.

That same day they headed back to the mountains.

❁❁❁

Time slipped by. The *queltehues* would fly over the house and then soar and disappear from sight for a while and then descend again. Salustio believed that the birds spoke to him and he would write things on pieces of paper.

"The birds know. They say that we have to be prepared, Clarisa. A terrible hurricane of evil beasts is coming."

She watched him out of the corner of her eye, pursed her lips and kept on working.

❁❁❁

Much more time went by. One morning when Salustio was seated facing the doorway of his house he saw him appear on the road.

He was a tall, thin man who walked as if the ground did not exist. He seemed transparent. And looked like a puppet dangling from the sky. He seemed filled with air. He resembled white smoke, like the dreams of the insane. He appeared to be very far away, approaching slowly but nonetheless always coming closer. His face was pale, his eyes blue and his hands were extremely slender. His cassock was dirty and full of patches. He wore a wooden cross around his neck. "He's just like Christ but with clothing that's been darned," Salustio thought as he continued to watch him.

When he reached the oak trees he stopped. He lowered a branch and grabbed a handful of *digueñes*. For a while he just looked at the ground. Then he seemed to rise, as he looked at the sky and next he stared at some faraway spot and sat down.

When Salustio reached the spot, the man was speaking to himself.

"The dead who don't come back are those who don't want to live the last night of their life. Those who do return do so because their last night was all white. Death carries them off asleep and they return to live another morning. The dead reach the open field and they seem surprised; they look in all directions, touch their hands, look for the kettle and ask: 'Where's my bed?' Nobody answers them because there's no one there. They start walking, looking for familiar faces, and sometimes they meet up with the dead who do not want to return, and the latter ask them to go back to take messages for them. There are also the dead who wake up in their beds and choose to stay awhile to see how others react to them. They feel neither sorrow nor anguish. They feel nothing. They remember, of course, and they speak to the living who are watching them, but the living cannot hear their words…Between life and death there is a spider web spun by unknown fingers…Only a few of the dead can traverse it. Going and coming…When time comes to an end everything else will also have ended. The web will break and the world will keep spinning devoid of life; it will take other roads, singing the song of the distant root and it will be lost forever in a bottomless pit that is located at the extreme left of the world of dreams."

"He's crazy," Salustio thought. He inclined his head a little in the hope that the man would look at him, but the man started to sing a song with other kinds of words. Salustio did not understand them, but it did not matter. His eyes were so blue and his face so beautiful that it made no difference what song he sang.

Salustio watched him fascinated. "He's God," he thought. But He was not God, even though he looked like Him.

Suddenly the man began to move his fingers and started to sketch circles in the air. Then he looked at Salustio.

"I've been searching for a village," he said.

"You've found it. It's called Tapihue. It's this one here," Salustio indicated as he pointed to his house.

"There's no church."

"There wasn't a house before either."

"You're right."

"It still needs about fifty adobe bricks."

"I've been walking for days. I'm tired," the man replied.

"I'm sure you are but we need you. We haven't been able to go to Mass for a long time. I've forgotten practically all the prayers. Besides, the *queltehues* say that a hurricane of evil beasts is coming. We have to be prepared, they say. You can't leave, father. Don't you like Tapihue? The place is full of *digueñes*, and there are also myrtle bushes. My wife's name is Clarisa. My son's name is José. Later on Vitoco and Enedina will come with their children who do not speak."

"This will be the church," the priest said, pointing to the dome created by the trees. He closed his eyes, made himself comfortable on the ground and fell asleep.

From the very beginning Clarisa thought he was strange. It bothered her that he ate so many *digueñes* and it annoyed her even more that he fed *digueñes* to the hen.

"He's going to make her sick. She's already acting strange. Talk to him, Salustio," she demanded.

"I'll speak to him about it," Salustio replied.

"You'll never say anything to him."

"Then don't ask me to."

"He makes me nervous when he starts talking to himself."

Clarisa kept spying on him to hear what he was saying, but she became irritated when she couldn't understand the words.

"You're not going to tell me that the prayers he says are from the Mass. He never says the Hail Mary nor any prayer seeking the intercession of our Holy Mother. And besides, he blesses himself backwards. First he says that there's the Son, then he says that there's the Father and he completely skips the Holy Spirit. I'm telling you, Salustio, this priest is from some other religion."

"Not all priests are alike."

"But they say Mass in the same way and you're not going to convince me that the Masses this priest says are like the others. He never stops eating *digueñes*, he takes communion by putting a handful of maqui in his mouth and he says Mass sitting in the last pew of the chapel. I'm getting a stiff neck and that song about the distant root is not a religious song. I know what I'm talking about, Salustio...Don't look at me like that. And don't start laughing. It would be better if you would explain to me why this priest sits in the last pew and doesn't stand at the altar like all the other priests."

"It's so that we look at the cross and not at him."

"What cross, if there isn't any."

It was then that Salustio began to doubt what he was saying. Actually, there was no cross in the chapel, but he was sure that for at least a moment there had been one. They had spoken about it with Francisco, which in fact was the name of the man who came walking toward their village as if the ground did not exist. He remembered that they were looking at the cross when the priest said that he liked it because it was a simple one and seemed to be made of air.

"Don't keep looking into space, answer me: what cross are you talking about if there isn't any?"

"The fact that you don't see it is one thing, but to say that it doesn't exist is something else. The fact is that the cross is made of air."

"And I suppose that the chalice that he raises and the bell that he says he rings are also made out of air?"

"They must be," replied Salustio, "because the bell sounds like birds singing and the chalice glitters as if it were on fire."

Clarisa, who was not convinced by his words, shouted at him:

"Look here, Salustio, you and that priest can laugh at whoever you want, but you're not going to tell me any tall tales. Today, and not a minute later, you're going to ask him," she said as she slammed the door behind her.

"What's the matter with her?" José asked when he saw her leave. "She's carrying one shoe in her hand."

"Don't speak to me. Can't you see that I'm made of air?"

José was going to ask him other questions but he continued to plane a piece of wood.

That afternoon Salustio went to speak to Francisco.

"Father," he began, "there are some things I need to ask you."

"Could you ask me a little later?"

"No."

"In that case go ahead and ask."

"Why is there no cross in the chapel?"

"Because José hasn't finished sanding down the wood."

"But you said that you liked the cross. Because it was simple and made of air, you said."

"That's right."

Salustio felt confused.

"And is there a chalice?"

"I don't remember."

"What do you mean you don't remember? You say Mass every day and you can't remember?"

"You go to Mass everyday too and you're not sure either."

"But is there or isn't there?"

"I don't know. Do you?"

"No, I don't know either."

"So then, what difference does it make?"

"And what about the bell?"

"There is no bell."

"But you say that you ring a bell."

"Almost everybody hears it."

"Clarisa doesn't."

"So, tell her there isn't any."

Salustio stuck his hands in his pocket, walked around the priest, looked at him and began to walk around him again before asking:

"Why do you say Mass sitting in the last pew and not in front of the altar like all the other priests?"

"Because there isn't any altar, Salustio."

Salustio kept looking at him; he heard the song of the distant root and did not dare to ask if it was a religious song.

"It's just a song, nothing else," said Francisco.

"How do you know what I'm thinking?"

"It's not that I know…"

Salustio kept looking at him, staring at him and holding his breath. Then he stepped back without taking his eyes off him. "He must be crazy, made of air, what do I know…He's a reincarnated *queltehue*, or the devil or a messenger who makes things up…Maybe he's a saint. Melania used to say that saints are magicians sent by God to make men better. But Clarisa will never understand…It's better not to even tell her that the priest is a messenger."

Clarisa was waiting for him at the door to their house. "Get ready, Salustio," he thought as he saw her, "here comes the barrage of questions What did he have to say about the chalice? And what about the cross? Did you ask him about the altar and about that song that isn't a religious one?"

"Help me pluck Josefa," the woman said.

Salustio said nothing. He remained quiet until she looked straight at him.

"What are you thinking about? Will you help me or not to pluck Josefa?"

Salustio took her by the hand, led her to the room and asked her to sit down. After a while he told her in a loud voice, louder than usual, not to dare pluck Josefa's feathers. Clarisa was frightened and preferred not to ask any questions.

"Have you looked at her eyes?" Salustio asked.

"No."

"Look at them."

The woman went out to the yard and tried to catch Josefa. The hen ran away from her.

"I just want to see your eyes," Clarisa shouted at the hen.

Josefa looked at her suspiciously but tiptoed back and allowed herself to be grabbed.

"Her eyes are the same as all the others," Clarisa said as she let the hen go.

"She's a hen of memory," Salustio answered from the doorway. "There are black hens, sad hens, good hens; and then there are hens of memory and those you can't eat."

❁❁❁

That night Salustio remembered the day they had gone to Sauzal. Clarisa woke him just before dawn.

"We've been living in this village for a long time and we have no neighbors other than that priest who isn't a priest. The hen that we brought with us we ate in August. You spoke about all the other people's hens that would be walking in our yards and now we don't have a single hen."

They were entering the village when a hen drew near the wagon and in one leap climbed on to Salustio's shoulder. He tried to get her off, but she stared at him without blinking and Salustio saw that she had tears in her eyes. They continued on the main street looking for the owner, stopping at several houses. The hen did not belong to anyone.

"She suddenly appeared out of nowhere," he grocer's wife said.

"If she doesn't belong to anyone, we'll take her with us," Salustio said, and so Josefa accompanied them to Tapihue.

"Why did we call her Josefa," Clarisa asked.

"Look at her eyes," Salustio answered.

"I've already seen them."

"Look at them again. The ones that are hens of memory have

33

eyes just like her. That's what the priest said, and they're always called Josefa."

"When José was born you said that if it was a girl we'd call her Josefa. And if the baby had been a girl…"

"The hen's name would be Chepa," Salustio said and he asked her to let him get some sleep.

"The priest is crazy and I think you are too," Clarisa insisted, but Salustio was already dreaming about what he had forgotten that day.

"Why do you skip the Holy Spirit," he asked. And in the dream the priest replied:

"I don't skip him. He's the one who skips me, but it's better for you not to dream about me. If tomorrow Clarisa asks you what you dreamed about, you're going to describe for her a solitary field, that has no beginning nor end, with bright stars filled with something like water, but that isn't water. You tell her you don't know what it is."

That is what the priest was saying to him when he awakened. Clarisa was already up. Josefa was next to the bed looking at him. Salustio believed that the hen was expressing her gratitude to him.

"Your name would have been Chepa," he said to her. The hen hopped up on his shoulder, stayed there for a while resting against Salustio's neck, and then jumped down and headed out of the room with her head held high.

❁❁❁

Enedina married Vitoco before she turned sixteen. From the very beginning they lived on the mountain in an abandoned house that Vitoco fixed up. They left Sauzal to get away from

Aunt Challo. Vitoco did not like her and Enedina was afraid of her. Doña Challo could see with only one eye and had a heart filled with bitterness. They had no other relatives. The two of them were cousins.

The children were born on the mountain. In the midst of an overwhelming silence. They came into the world like little fish, with their green eyes opened wide. Without crying. Enedina wiped them and wrapped them in a blanket. Then she sat beside each newborn waiting for him to cry. "Cry, my child," she would implore between pangs of sharp pain that she kept experiencing from giving birth. "Cry, my child." Her children never cried. They simply looked at her with their big intelligent eyes. Then they would fall asleep with their eyes open.

After six were born Vitoco said that it was necessary to baptize them and that Salustio and Clarisa would be the godparents.

That very morning they went to look for them and together they departed for Sauzal. There they inquired about a priest. Someone pointed to the church. They knocked on the door and a priest appeared. He had been up all night. His eyes were swollen and his cracked lips were encircled by a coffee-colored substance. His shirt was unbuttoned and he wore a silver cross on his chest.

"We came from the mountains to have our children baptized," Vitoco explained.

"What children?" the priest asked.

"Those in the wagon."

"How many are there?"

"Six."

"And the godparents?"

"Those two who have come with us: Salustio and Clarisa," replied Vitoco as he pointed them out to the priest.

"I can't. It's not allowed. The children have to have different godparents. Two for each child. Besides, they have to be newborns. The ones I see there are grown children. Unbaptized Moors. That's what they are. Unbaptized children. They're going to go to Limbo when they die and will never get to heaven and God will punish the two of you for not bringing them on time to be baptized and with proper godparents just as God demands. Now go back, return to your homes and meditate. Pray. Three Our Fathers, two Hail Marys…"

The priest was going to continue talking but Enedina interrupted him and said, in a voice that no one had ever heard her use before:

"Your God is a sick god. You are very sick. My children will grow up without having been baptized and neither your hand nor your consecrated oil will save them from the inferno that is this life. You're the devil's priest!"

She was beside herself with anger. She seemed to be someone else.

Vitoco did not recognize her, and Salustio and Clarisa looked at her as if they had never seen her before.

The priest looked at her with eyes filled with fury and his face began to tremble.

"Get out. Get out of here," he said pushing them towards the wagon. He tripped on a rock and fell flat on his face and even on the ground he kept shouting at them with his eyes popping out of his head, his hands trembling more and more and his voice exploding in anger.

"Get out!"

From the wagon they could hear the door slam.

They set out again in silence. Vitoco unenthusiastically prodded the ox.

"There aren't any other churches in these parts. They're going to end up in Limbo and you'll be to blame for it. One shouldn't yell at priests, and, on top of everything, you insulted him."

"I got upset and lost my head," Enedina offered as an excuse.

"I hope you get your head on straight once and for all."

From that time on Enedina hardly spoke and their lives evolved in a silence intensified only by that of the children, who were growing up mute, playing their animal games and looking at the mountain as if they were birds.

When they moved to Tapihue, Clarisa tried to teach them to speak but they refused.

"They haven't received God's grace. That's why. He has punished them."

"And you think that God goes around taking his revenge out on children? You think God punishes children because one of the devil's priests refused to baptize them?" José asked.

"What do you know about the devil's priests! You'd better bless yourself. Children have to be baptized so that they can enter a state of grace and be like the rest of us. Salustio and I will be the godparents," Clarisa said, and that crazy priest will baptize them.

✿✿✿

"What do you want at this late hour?" Francisco asked her. She explained it all to him.

At first Francisco did not want to. He said that it wasn't even proved that grace comes from being baptized and, in any case, you don't learn to speak by being in a state of grace.

"But you're a priest and you can't refuse to baptize Christians," Clarisa insisted and then asked in the same breath: "Do you know how to baptize?"

"Everybody knows," he said.
"But do you baptize like every other priest or like the way you say Mass?"

"Like all the priests in the world...Don't look at me like that. There's only one way to baptize. Bring the children and the godparents, have everyone come, and tell Josefa to come too."

The six children stood facing the imaginary altar. Salustio and Clarisa positioned themselves just a step in front of them, just as they had seen people do at a baptism in Sauzal. Vitoco and Enedina stood behind the children. José sat in one of the pews in the middle and Josefa wandered around.

Francisco remained leaning against the frame of the door. No one knew what to do. Nobody moved. They didn't know whether the ceremony had already begun or not. Suddenly the priest began to sing the song of the distant root and while singing, with eyes intensely blue, infinite and sparkling, he approached the children, who stared the way simpletons do, as if nothing that was happening around them had the least bit of importance.

A tepid air entered the chapel and left it insulated from the morning's cold. Then the earth moved and Clarisa and Salustio, Enedina and Vitoco, Josefa, José and the children all started to levitate. It wasn't that they were flying; it was simply the fact that the earth was sinking. The priest placed his hands on the oldest child's head, closed his eyes and said:

"No one knows why you refuse to talk. Maybe you were born tired. The things of this life are very strange. Maybe you have nothing to say. It could be for all of these reasons because in life everything is relative. Clarisa asked me to give you a name that you already have. Therefore I am baptizing you Martín, Raúl, Florín, Bernardo, Juan and Primitivo, in the name of the Son, the Father, Amen."

Then he opened his eyes and continued:

"Your parents are Vitoco and Enedina. Your godparents are Salustio and Clarisa. My name is Francisco. We don't have surnames. You're free. You can change your name and your parents and godparents whenever you choose to do so…May you be filled with God's grace even though you never learn to speak."

That is what he said. Shortly after he closed his eyes again, bowed and walked toward the door.

Clarisa, who up until that moment had seemed as if she were asleep, realized what had taken place. "The Devil's priest, this crazy priest, he's an impostor," she said. "That's not the way you baptize people. Without even water on their heads or salt on their foreheads, what a phony priest. They're going to remain mute forever and God is going to punish all of us for attending false baptisms."

"This isn't a false baptism," Clarisa. "Besides, God does not punish," Francisco said to her in passing.

"You devil," she shouted as she looked for Salustio's eyes.

"They're already baptized," he said smiling.

"They're possessed," she answered back. "Possessed and mute."

Salustio looked at her puzzled.

"We're all condemned. That's what we are," thought Clarisa at that moment.

"Condemned…?" asked Salustio as he looked toward the tops of the pine trees.

Clarisa gave a start.

"No one is condemned, woman. No one," Salustio added.

"You're a devil, too, just like the priest!" Clarisa concluded.

"It's your eyes" he replied." They're transparent and your thoughts give you away.

They did not take up the issue again.

The children continued mute and Clarisa blamed Josefa.

❂❂❂

One afternoon the people of Tapihue set to thinking as they sat in front of their houses. They were sad. They all had similar thoughts, but they said nothing. They believed that there were too few of them and that they did not constitute a village.

Vitoco felt that he had lost faith in the priest. It was because of the baptism which did not serve any purpose. He found Salustio to be different ever since Francisco arrived. He was no longer the Salustio of the mountains; he had a strange light in his eyes and he said things that Vitoco did not understand at all. Once he tried to tell Enedina that something was wrong with Salustio: he spoke in half sentences and left the other half for his listener to figure out. He tried to talk to her about it but he ended up by not saying anything. He had also heard José say that Salustio and Francisco talked to the *queltehues*. José explained to him that it was the priest who talked to the birds and that Salustio simply believed he heard them and drew crazy things on pieces of paper. Vitoco was left even more confused when José told him that Clarisa was frightened because Salustio became angry when she tried to slit Josefa's throat to make a *cazuela*. All of this worried Vitoco. "It must be what God wants," he thought as he watched Josefa peck at the ground.

Clarisa felt that practically everything was missing in Tapihue.

She was convinced that the priest, the only thing typical of a village that they had, was crazy. Nonetheless, there was something about the priest she liked. She did not know what it was. That is why she kept going to Mass. She would leave the church angry but on the following day she always went back. She did not take communion. No, that she would not do. Not with maqui, no. If she did she would be condemned for eternity.

"If you think you're going to be condemned don't go," Salustio would say to her. And then she would explain to him that for the purpose of not committing a sacrilege any Mass is good enough and that when the priest raised the chalice made of air and said "everything is relative, even God and Death are nothing more than a form of oblivion," she always invoked the Lamb of God who takes away the sins of the world and promised to say an Our Father and three Hail Marys.

Clarisa believed that in spite of the priest and the way he said Mass, in spite of the few residents, and how nervous that hen would get, Tapihue could not be compared to the solitude of the mountains, and even when she had imagined that they would live in a village full of *comadres*, with lots of streets and a dentist, a church with an altar and a golden chalice and even a plaza full of children flying kites, she recognized that she was happy there. "I feel alive," she thought and stared at the road.

Salustio believed that given time they would eventually have all they needed. José grew like a vine. He was already asking questions that men ask. Salustio imagined him leaving the village and coming back with a wife and grandchildren to be named by him. The first one would be called Abel. Abelina if it was a girl. The only thing he asked was that their eyes not be green like those of the children. He would buy them a dog and they would call the dog Florián, and Clarisa would chase him with her broom.

Tapihue would grow like a eucalyptus tree, he thought, and he would be the village elder who would tell things to people, give them advice, and he would be the founder, and when the moment to depart arrived, he, older than the oldest in the village, would leave smiling, and at his burial they would have an orchestra and the bishop would speak. Because at some time in the future the bishop would come to bless Tapihue; bishops do that sort of thing in all the villages that appear on maps. Tapihue would be on a map, he was sure of it, and all of this was thanks to him, who ultimately would be called Don Salustio, and they would dedicate a statue to him. "One for me and another for my father," he thought as he looked toward the tops of the pine trees. His eyes were full of tears, but only Josefa, who was watching him, was aware that he was crying.

Enedina was sad. As always.

Francisco was asleep dreaming of the sea.

❂❂❂

It was close to four o'clock in the afternoon when they saw him coming.

In one hand he carried a broken kite and in the other a small suitcase.

"Another crazy one," Clarisa thought. The others watched him without shifting their gaze.

When the man was directly opposite the priest he introduced himself.

"Esmeraldo…I'm a dentist and my name is Esmeraldo, but my grandfather called me Rómulo and sometimes he called me Juvenal. Shortly before he died he said that the priest who baptized me was in a hurry and finished without giving me a name.

In any case, I like Esmeraldo…

He spoke slowly, almost in a whisper, looking off to the side. His face was burned by the sun and his jaws were rigid. He seemed to be afraid. The people of the village did not ask any questions. He kept looking at them. After a while he said that everyone had left; that one morning he awoke and discovered that they were no longer there. Not even the ox. He was completely alone, he said. They had even taken his pincers with them. They left him a letter, but he refused to open it.

"I've got it in my pocket," he said. Francisco asked him to show it to him and the dentist handed him a yellowed envelope.

"It's blank," the priest said, showing him the letter.

"Maybe the words were erased," the dentist replied.

"When did they leave?" the priest asked.

"Years ago," he said, and then he asked if he could stay with them.

"Now we have a dentist," Salustio said that night. He was happy. "Tomorrow I'm going to have my tooth pulled."

"He doesn't have a pincers," Clarisa said.

"I'll take mine."

"Yours isn't the kind dentists use."

"It doesn't matter. It pulls just the same."

"It's your tooth. If you get chills and fever work it out with the priest. But if you die…Salustio, if you die, I'll kill you."

Salustio went to see him the following morning.

The dentist was living in the priest's house until his own was completed.

"He's sleeping," said Francisco.

"Wake him up, father. Tell him his first customer is here." Shortly after Esmeraldo appeared. He entered yawning.

"Is it true you want to have a tooth pulled…? It's no big deal, but I don't have my pincers."

"I brought my own."

"Let me see them," he said, and Salustio handed them to him.

"They'll do," he declared after weighing them in his hand. They went into the kitchen. He asked him to sit on the floor and open his mouth.

"The tooth's bad. It's going to hurt. Do you have any brandy?"

"Just wine."

"How much?"

"A carafe."

"Bring it here."

Salustio returned with the carafe and he began to drink the wine as if it were water. Within a few minutes he was drunk and when the dentist asked him to open his mouth, he began to sing the song of the distant root and his eyes danced as he sang. The priest had to help. An hour later the dentist had the tooth in his hand.

"You smell of wine," Clarisa said to him.

"He already pulled it."

"Do you have chills and fever?"

"I'm tired," he said as he fell asleep.

❂❂❂

Esmeraldo followed the priest around like a lap dog. And besides this, he ate *digueñes*, he took *maqui* for communion, and skipped the Holy Spirit, but he never learned the song of the distant root. Twice he went to Sauzal to buy a pincers and both times he came back saying there were none to be found. One day he confessed that he liked speaking with Francisco more than he liked being a dentist, and that he hated his profession so much that he had refused to practice it. He ended up admitting that Salustio's tooth was the only tooth he had pulled in his entire life.

Whenever he spoke of his life he said that it was a sad one.

"Ever since I met Fidelina, father," he said one day to Francisco.

"Your wife?"

"Yes…She told me that my heart was paralyzed and since that time all of my memories were erased. I was thirty years old when she came into my life. I saw her father and I was smitten forever. Insanity. I had been sleeping for almost an hour. When I woke up she was there looking at me. She threw water in my face, I think, so that I would wake up."

"We got married in Sauzal and went to Molco to live. That was when I told her I was a dentist. She believed me in spite of the fact that I had ugly teeth, just like they are now. Only once did she ask me why I didn't replace them with false ones. I don't remember what I told her. She never asked me again…She liked dresses. She was always asking me to buy her a new dress and I always did."

"Were you rich?"

"The day I met her I had a suitcase filled with money that I kept under my bed. But whatever happened before then I forgot. I don't know where the money came from. I told her it was money I inherited from my Uncle Alfonso Luna. A name I made up. And we lived on that money. We bought the house in Molco and the ox. I always left the house early in the morning."

"I'm going to pull teeth," I'd tell her, "but she was always asleep and never asked me anything. I always traveled the road between Molco and Unihue…I'd leave just so I could think about her…I loved her and I still love her, father. When I realized that she was with another man while I was gone pulling imaginary teeth, I thought that I was going to lose my mind, but I didn't say anything to her. I smelled the other man on her body, but her smell was stronger and I just forgot about it all."

"Do you have children?"

"She had one. His name is Fidel."

"Why are you crying?"

"Because I can't forget her."

"Did she die?"

"I don't know…They took everything. I woke up that morning and there wasn't one thing left in the house. Not even my pincers and my apron."

"Couldn't you have dreamed it all?"

"No, father, Fidelina was real, and Abel, her retarded brother, and Juana, who took care of him and hugged him at night…All of it was real. The ox too."

Esmeraldo often went to Sauzal. "I like to sit in the plaza," he would say, but that is not why he went. He went to see if he could find Fidelina.

One day he returned saying that there was a sadness floating in the air, that he noticed it on the faces of the people, he said, and he asked the priest to explain it to him.

The priest spoke to him about the sadness. He explained that it could be found everywhere, beneath the bedspreads, stuffed into the pillows, hanging between the branches of the pine trees, floating in the cracks of the walls, running through the wood of the crosses.

"It comes from the cities," he said. And then he pointed out that it was impossible to conceive life without sadness; that women with the sadness stop being women and they become balls of wool and sleep balled up at the foot of their beds, hoping that the sadness will go away, but the sadness is never the one who departs. It's necessary to let go of the sadness but it's almost impossible to do so. He said that men cry with their faces covered by a hat. He spoke of the sadness announced by the *queltehues*:

"That's what you saw in Sauzal. It's a sadness that's capable of penetrating even the bones of living and dead souls leaving everything wrapped within a painful heaviness, leaving children frightened and animals shaking. It's the sadness of the end, the sadness that no one wants to understand, not even after they've died, the sadness that leaves everything filled with loneliness."

"And before, when you were young, father, did you sometimes feel the sadness?"

"Yes. Once. I was nineteen years old. Read this paper," he said, and he handed him a yellowed piece of paper that he took from his pocket.

The dentist started to read: "much longer ago than I probably think, because when I'm drunk I can't think at all; hidden in the drop of a word, with no more light than a lamp lit memory, with no more dreams than the dreams of mornings, suspended on a faith that I no longer have, holding on to the skirts of a God I no longer believe in…"

He was about to keep reading, when he raised his head and saw Clarisa standing opposite them; then he grew silent.

"I heard everything," she said. "Salustio can say whatever he wants, but you, you're no priest; and you, don't you go looking at me like that because I also know that you're no dentist. That's the truth of it," she said without stopping to catch her breath as she turned and walked away.

That afternoon she told Salustio to wake up.

"How am I supposed to wake up when I'm not even asleep?"

"I'm not saying you're asleep. I'm telling you to wake up once and for all and realize that any so-and-so can come to this village saying he's a priest or a dentist and you believe him. To-morrow if a purple dress arrives you'll believe it's the bishop. And you know why I'm telling you all this? Stop looking at the ceiling! You know why? Because the priest has made him stupid."

"Made who stupid?"

"Who do you think? The dentist. I caught them. The dentist had that dumb look on his face as he read a love letter the priest handed to him. It's all there. In the letter. It said that he's a drunk and that when he's drunk he stops thinking and that he has no faith whatsoever, and that he lives hanging on to a God that wears skirts, and that he doesn't even believe in that God. Are you listening to me, Salustio? A God that wears skirts…Drunken priests are not priests and that maqui that he distributes is blessed by a crazy man, and you go and receive communion, and the poor children and Vitoco and Enedina receive communion, and you open your mouths without realizing what you're doing…If you fall asleep now I'll…" Clarisa threatened him. "Look at me, Salustio!"

"Everything is relative," he said.

"Relative…"

"It can either be or not be."

"But right now it is. Don't pretend you're asleep. I know you. You're not tired, Salustio."

✪✪✪

Salustio was painting the door of his house when Filuca arrived. He did not hear her approach until her body was so close to his that he could smell her breath of cummin seed. Only then did he turn around and see her. She was tall and thin. Her face had something strange about it and so did her being there. She resembled the dead a little, but she was alive and seemed willing to remain there forever.

"What's your name?"

Silence.

"Where are you from?"

Again, silence…Big, round, dark eyes were looking at him without blinking.

"Who are you talking to," Clarisa asked from the kitchen.

"To a girl who just arrived and doesn't respond to my questions. She doesn't have a name and doesn't come from anywhere."

"Everybody has a name," Clarisa shouted.

"But she doesn't say anything. She's like a statue. She stares and doesn't move. She got here so fast it was almost as if she flew. She's wearing a silver bracelet on her hand. A thick bracelet."

"What color are her eyes?"

"Dark."

"And her hands?"

"White."

"Tell her to raise one of them."

"Raise one of your hands," Salustio asked her, but she did not react.

"Is she conscious," Clarisa asked.

"Sometimes I think you're stupid. Didn't I tell you that she's been standing in front of me without moving?"

"Is she breathing?"

"Why don't you come here and see for yourself?"

"Because I've just started to make the *cazuela*."

"Don't you lay a hand on Josefa! Come here!"

Clarisa stepped outside, wiping her hands on a rag. She kept looking at the young girl for a while.

"What's your name?" she asked her.

The girl, who was no more than about eighteen, remained unintimidated, and after a bit she gestured with her hand and showed Clarisa her bracelet.

"She's a mute," Clarisa said. "Go get Francisco."

The priest looked at her carefully and asked if she knew the song of the distant root.

"She can't speak or hear. How is she supposed to know that pagan song?"

"It's possible that she remembers it. The *queltehues* say she does. And besides, last night they announced that she would come. Her name is Filuca. That's what the birds said. They also sang that she's been wandering for a long time. She doesn't have anyone. She's going to stay here. She can cook and she's a good person. I'll take care of her. That's what the *queltehues* want."

"But she's a woman and you're a priest. Priests and women don't mix. That's what the Bible says. It's a sin," said Clarisa, staring at Salustio.

"Didn't you say that he's a drunk and a fake priest?" Salustio asked.

"Do what you want. We're all condemned anyway, even Josefa," she said as she went back into the house slamming the door behind her.

Filuca stayed. She lived in the priest's house and slept on a bed that José made for her. In the beginning the people of the village looked at each other without saying anything. The priest, through signs, explained to Filuca that she too could take communion. When Filuca approached the altar that now existed, without understanding what was happening and ate the handful of *maqui*, the people looked at each other again. Salustio sang the song of the distant root. The others followed his example. Clarisa bowed her head and Josefa knelt down under a pew and, without anyone seeing her, made the sign of the cross.   "Mutes can't take communion," Clarisa said that night.

"Yes they can."

"And their sins?"

"They don't have any," said Salustio and he turned over.

Filuca knew the hours and the days. Her life went by as if the house were filled with calendars and clocks. She would get up at six in the morning; sprinkle the floor with water, sweep it and then light the fire. When the priest came out of his room, the water was already boiling, and a steaming cup of tea and hot bread were waiting for him.

No one showed her how to do this. She knew these things simply because she had to. She could read Francisco's thoughts. Since coming to the house she did the same things that he did, as if she had been the one who taught him. The ears of corn cooked every Saturday, the *mote* with coriander on Sundays and even the bowl filled with *digueñes* on Thursday afternoons. Everything just the way the priest liked it.

She was clean and silent.

At night she would sit by the fireplace and there she would remain with her hands clasped over her stomach, looking at the red coals. Silent. As if she were not even there.

Whenever Francisco started to speak, she raised her head and looked at him. The priest would tell her the kind of stories in which things and people are what they are not. In Francisco's stories everything happened the other way around. Death was life and life was an invention. Women were vegetables or sparrows or vegetables were rain, but rain fell from the earth and mountains arose backwards, and no animal lived in the hills because some of them were made of fire, and oxen swam in the sea where green and luminous stars floated.

"Like fireflies," the priest said.

Enedina was the thought of an angel who was never born, but who nonetheless was buried the day she died. It was a burial without any prayers. The priest did not feel like praying and the others did not know how.

Filuca never took her eyes off the priest's face. She looked at him as if she understood and, when he stopped speaking, she would touch one of his hands and he would start another story. Then Filuca's face would light up and this is how they would spend hours and hours, until she would fall asleep, always at two in the morning.

Whenever anyone came to the house she would disappear. She never opened the door and the priest never spoke about her. People in the village saw her on Sundays when she approached to take communion and then she would hurry back to her pew. There she remained for a while looking at Francisco and then she would get up and leave.

Clarisa came to believe that she did not exist.

"We invented her," she said one day.

One night Filuca dreamed that she woke up and was looking for Francisco throughout the house. It was completely dark. She groped around looking for him. She searched the corners, under the beds, inside the closet, between the sheets, she even looked for him on the ceiling. But he was no where to be found. She checked the beams with a broom handle just in case he was perched up there. Then she went into the street and without knocking, entered houses where people were still sleeping. There she checked everything once again. She woke her neighbors up.

And still he was no where to be found. Next she climbed up to the top of the pine trees, shook the branches, but he was not there either. She climbed down and looked among the myrtle bushes. She entered the waters of the stream, looked at the sky and the earth below and searched for him on the horizon. He was not there. It was then that a howl like that of an animal emanated from her throat.

The priest approached her bed and woke her.

"You dreamed that I had died, but I'm here," he said to her and he got into bed beside her and the two bodies fused so gently that they seemed to have always lived like that, and they stayed this way the rest of the night, rolled up in a ball at the end of the bed, touching, recognizing each other, silent, scarcely moving, in no more of a hurry than time that had almost stopped, feeling no more anxiety than that of a contented bird, with no other destiny than that of loving one another forever, silent, in the midst of a sleeping village that perhaps was never going to wake up.

❂❂❂

Jose had turned fifteen and he knew his days in Tapihue were numbered. Clarisa taught him to read and write and Francisco had told him that they were from a country whose cities were formed by many Tapihues, one standing alongside the other, and by many sad people who walked as if they were doing it from memory.

He wanted to leave Tapihue. He had no friends. No wife. Martín, Vitoco's eldest son, was fifteen like him, but he lived in a silent world, and every time he tried to speak to him, ask him things, the boy simply walked away without saying anything, looking at him with those eyes of his, not making any noise, without trying to explain with his hands, without a single part of his face moving.

One day he told him that he awoke consumed by passion, that he had dreamed of a naked woman, that in the dream he was rubbing his body against the woman's and that they ended up making love on the floor of a room. He told him that when he woke up his penis was as hard as a rock and he went out into the patio half naked and chased the sow until he caught hold of her and there, behind the myrtle bushes, he tried to imagine that the sow was the woman in his dream, but the sow screamed furiously and, even though he succeeded in calming the heat of his passion, he swore to himself that the next time it would be with a real woman...The boy kept looking at him as if José had not said anything to him and then he walked away enveloped in a cloud of tranquility.

"I dream about women," he said to Salustio one night.

"You're going on sixteen."

"But here there aren't any."

"I understand."

"In Sauzal I'll find work."

By the following week he was gone. Clarisa did not even have a chance to grieve about his departure because that same night Enedina went crazy.

❂❂❂

It was close to ten o'clock when Vitoco came running. His face was distorted and he could barely speak. He uttered a few disconnected words that Salustio and Clarisa could not make out.

"Five hens...She says...Five children."

"Speak more clearly," Salustio asked him, but Vitoco could

not articulate complete sentences and he kept on perspiring. Clarisa gave him a glass of wine.

"Sit down and rest."

Salustio left to see what was happening. On the way he thought about the first letter that José would write. "I hope he finds a girl so that he'll get married and produce lots of grandchildren."

He entered Enedina's house without knocking and saw her. She was sitting on the bed with a lost look on her face, moving her hands through the air in a zigzag fashion.

"Five wagons all patched up, five speckled hens, five lives, five deaths, five priests with five heads at five Masses with less than five crosses on five infinite Thursdays, five minutes that are almost eternal, that five gods demanded after the last five days, from the first five women married to five bad men, with more than five children, all of them deaf and dumb, yellow, with five different voices…"

She continued on and on. Everything was in fives.

"Enedina," Salustio said, shaking her by the shoulders. "Stop talking. Listen to me Enedina. It's me. Salustio."

It was no use. The woman continued to move her hands in front of her eyes that had a lost look about them, speaking about a whole bunch of things, all of them based on the number five, while her six children watched without moving, crammed into a corner of the room, silent and afraid.

"She's gone crazy," Salustio said and he left to get the priest.

Francisco was speaking with a *queltehue* when Salustio arrived.

"What's going on? You've come running and you've got the look of a mad man," the priest said.

"It's Enedina, father, she won't stop talking. She sees everything in fives. She seems lost and doesn't stop moving her hands. The way a dancer does but she's not dancing. She's sitting on the bed and the children are watching her from a corner of the room. Please, father, you've got to come with me."

"I'm a priest...if she's sick in the head..."

"Come anyway."

The *queltehue* remained looking at the two of them until they entered Enedina's house.

"Five offenses one after the other, five bad priests, each five minutes a minute of five eternities, five empty words after five mornings of sorrow, five years of life for a whole life of five consecutive years..."

The priest pulled up a stool and sat down next to the woman.

"Tell me everything. Keep talking," he asked her and he spent close to an hour listening to the litany of fives. Then he got up and asked Salustio about Vitoco.

"He's at my house." Clarisa gave him a glass of wine. "He couldn't even speak, but what's wrong with Enedina? She's gone crazy, hasn't she?"

"There's nothing crazy about her. She's sick from grief."

"But if this business of fives is not craziness then what is, father?"

"Salustio, this is grief and it's the grief of fives, the grief of tens is worse. Go get Vitoco."

"Vitoco is afraid."

"Bring him anyway."

Shortly after Salustio returned. He came with Vitoco trailing behind him.

"He's drunk. Clarisa gave him all the wine we had in the house."

"It doesn't matter. Sit him down near the bed."

"But he's falling down drunk."

"He doesn't have to say anything, just be here," Francisco said and he approached the children, and put his hands on Martín's head.

"You're going to approach your mother and you're going to say "Mom", Francisco said to him.

The boy drew back completely and tried to escape between the priest's legs. Francisco grabbed him by the hair and dragged him to Enedina's bedside. He sat him down on the stool where he had been sitting and in a voice that was not his, in a voice so strong and so powerful that it seemed to come from a much older world, he commanded him:

"Say "Mom" to her!"

"Mom" the boy said and he returned to his corner with the same inexpressive look that he always had.

"Salustio's vision became blurred. Enedina suddenly ended her litany of fives and closed her eyes.

"She's asleep," Francisco said and then he withdrew.

❂❂❂

Two years passed since José's departure. Clarisa had a hard time getting used to it but José wrote once a week. In addition, he had visited them on several occasions. Chickens, pork sausage, two roosters, three hens, a pig. These were just some of the gifts he brought them. On his last trip he brought María. Salustio kept looking at her stomach in the secret hope that she was pregnant so that they could start having grandchildren, but María was too young. She was the same age as José.

"Be patient," José said to him. "When they make me the head lathe operator we'll get married." Clarisa's anxiety began to grow and it penetrated every corner of her body when five months went by and they still received no news from José.

"He must have changed jobs. He's probably in some far off village," Salustio said trying to calm her.

"There are post offices everywhere. And the *queltehues* told you that we had to be prepared."

"Birds don't speak, Clarisa. I made that up."

"You didn't make anything up. The *queltehues* speak to the priest and to you too. I've seen what you draw. They speak of that hurricane of wicked beasts, they speak of fear, of death...I'm afraid, Salustio."

"Try to sleep."

"I can't. I'm filled with anxiety. Tomorrow I'm going to go look for him."

"Lets go with the priest. Let's go with Vitoco and Enedina. With the dentist and the children. The whole village will go," Salustio said, but he could not convince her.

"I know how to do these things myself," she said and set out to look for her son.

Three days went by, then a week, then two, and Clarisa did not return. However, Salustio was calm.

"Go look for her," the priest suggested.

"Why?"

"So she'll come back."

"She'll be back. I know my wife better than you, father."

That afternoon she returned. She arrived in a wagon prodding an old, mud covered ox who seemed to be living out the final moments of his life.

"José isn't in Sauzal. He's not in Unihue. He's not in Santa Clara. He's not in Molco. He's not in Chanco. In Sauzal they told me that he got married last year. But they're no longer there. I couldn't find out anything else about them. The people there speak very little and the children walk around frightened. I'm going to keep looking for them. I bought the wagon and Fulgencio. That's his name. He's a little old but willing. I'm going to travel every road on this earth until I find them. The earth just doesn't go around swallowing up other people's sons, nor their wives."

That's what she said. Then she climbed down from the wagon, went into the house, sat down next to the brazier and there she remained the whole night, silent and crying.

Salustio became frightened. He had never seen her like that. He remembered that the dentist said he also knew a little about medicine. Maybe there was some tranquilizer, some remedy for grief, something…And he went to look for him.

The dentist accompanied him as far as the house, glad to be able to help in whatever way he could.

That was when he saw the ox.

"Fulgencio!" he shouted and he threw himself on the ox kissing him on the neck as if he were a woman. Fulgencio looked at him and several large, heavy tears flowed from the eyes of the thin, worn-out ox.

Salustio did not understand what was going on, but he kept silent waiting for the dentist and the ox to finish caressing each other. "Only God knows what has happened to this man in life," he thought. He made no comments nor did he ask any questions.

"Fulgencio," the dentist mumbled in a broken voice. "Fulgencio, my friend, why did you leave like that when you were the only one who understood my broken heart."

Fulgencio looked at him and in the eyes of the aged ox it was obvious that he understood, but he said nothing, or maybe he said something, but Salustio only heard the words mixed with the dentist's sobbing.

"Maybe a *queltehue* can explain what's happening," he thought, "but I think Clarisa is right: this dentist must be crazy." He was thinking about all of this when he saw the knife go in and it sounded to him like the way lightning sounds when it cuts through the heavens.

The dentist fell to the ground and there he remained, with his eyes open, staring like the dead do with that far away look in their eyes. His pupils remained glued to the sky.

Salustio felt his body become paralyzed while Fulgencio, bending his front legs, knelt down next to Esmeraldo and lowered his head: "Our Father who art in heaven," he murmured. Salustio ran to the priest's house, tripping over the stones along the way and shouting:

"He killed himself, he killed himself! Francisco, Enedina, Vitoco, come all of you! He's dead. It was the knife. And the ox is praying."

The priest came running out of his house. Vitoco and Enedina did too. The children, Filuca, the pigs, the ducks, the hens, all came. The whole village went to see what was happening. Clarisa was the only one who stayed where she was.

"What's going on?" the priest asked, and Salustio, who suddenly became mute, managed only to point with his finger toward the spot where Esmeraldo's body lay.

On the following day they buried him. While Vitoco and Salustio shoveled dirt on the grave, Francisco said prayers for the dead.

"We are an addition and a subtraction. Sometimes Zero turns up and it is then that we must depart. Those who commit suicide understand this immediately and do not wait for any other decisions, neither from Destiny nor from God. Point Zero in man is an abyss where the body becomes smoke, the mind becomes air and the soul remains covered by a blanket of sorrow that is so pervasive it wipes away all memory in one stroke. The only thing that remains is the raw naked soul, filled with an interminable insomnia, with all hope of rest lost, and with the image of life clouded.

"Point Zero cannot be resisted by man. The sea stops moving. Birds come to a halt and are left embalmed and silent. Rivers no longer flow. Time comes to an end, tree tops remain silent, the crests of hills go into hiding, nature no longer breathes. And it is then that man knows he is trapped between the beginning and the end. That is what happened to the dentist. It was not the knife. It was not the sadness running through his existence. It was not his encounter with Fulgencio. It was Point Zero. God knows all of this and those who take their life know that God knows. That is why they go to Him with their faces so peaceful looking. God looks straight at them and after a while He begins to cry, and for an entire day, one day of this life, God lives His own Point Zero. But He does not commit suicide, because it serves no purpose for Him. At this very moment the dentist is watching God's tears flow. Amen."

The people of the village returned to their homes with bowed heads. The priest's words had made their hearts tremble. A sudden silence fell upon the village that entered through the tree tops, penetrated everything along its path until it made its way beneath the earth silencing roots, worms and rocks.

Clarisa remained by the brazier.

"Is the funeral over?" she asked when she saw Salustio enter.

"God is crying."

"It's because of Point Zero."

"And you, how do you know if you didn't go?"

✪✪✪

Two nights later, while everyone was asleep, someone entered the village. He walked slowly. He was filled with fatigue and with an endless sadness. He went directly to the tomb of the dentist. There he knelt down and began to cry. Afterwards he got up and gathered several myrtle branches.

"So they'll keep you company. So there will be life in the earth that covers you," he said as he scattered the branches on the ground.

Josefa had heard noises and when she saw him enter the village she followed him.

She watched what was going on in complete silence so that he would not hear her. She never forgot what she heard there and fell in love with Fulgencio's sad face as she had never fallen in love before with anyone and to such an extent that she swore if Clarisa wrung her neck, she would die for him. "Like the Christians for Christ," she thought and kept watching.

"You will continue to wander through solitary fields looking for your unfaithful Fidelina. You will continue to extract the teeth of the wind and recognize the unknown dead," the ox said and then he prayed the Our Father.

"You must be looking for poor Abel, Juana and Fidel. Who knows where you are, Esmeraldo. Who knows whether it's true that whole thing about Point Zero and whether or not you've seen God cry. Here we are left filled with questions. With our hearts broken just like you…Blessed be your name, may your kingdom come, forgive us our sins; don't let us fall into temptation. Deliver us from evil," he said. Then he stood up and headed in the direction he came from. Josefa followed on tiptoe just a few meters behind.

Fulgencio withdrew slowly. As he walked along the road he left a trail of tears. He stopped at the end of the street, looked up, raised his mud covered tail, breathed deeply and started to fly.

Josefa opened her eyes as she had never opened them in her entire life while she flapped her wings, determined to rise and lose herself in the heavens until she caught up with Fulgencio. But she had never flown before and fell to the ground, and there she remained shrunken in sorrow and powerlessness.

✿✿✿

On the following day Clarisa said that the hen was limping. "Old age is catching up with her. Given all of the terrible things that are happening to us, we're in no position to take care of an old hen. Besides, that ox disappeared after the burial. The times that the *queltehue* spoke so much about are already upon us, Salustio. The hurricane of evil beasts has already taken place. God only knows what it will all be like, but look what's happened to José. He's disappeared. As if he were swallowed up by the earth. As if he had never been born. No one has seen him. His boss in Sauzal denies everything. As if José had told us nothing but lies. 'Nobody by the name of José has ever worked for me.' That's what he said. He's not in jail, nor in the morgue, he's not in any hospital, he's not anywhere. The authorities check their lists and say: 'No, your son's not here.' How do you explain this, Salustio? José couldn't have forgotten us. Something happened to him."

"I don't understand," Salustio said. "Francisco says that evil forces have come, but this whole business about José I don't understand at all. Nor what's happened with the ox. Maybe he went to look for José. That ox had a strange look in his eyes. Did you notice?"

"You always say that the animals have a strange look in their eyes. Like Josefa. I took a good long look in her eyes and they seemed like all the others to me. She's gotten old, Salustio. And we don't have enough to feed ourselves. The priest said that in Sauzal they're running out of food. Can we kill her?"

"Okay," he said and left the room murmuring: "She's old. She's tired."

Josefa guessed that she would die that day but it no longer mattered to her. When Clarisa wrung her neck, she thought she would die with dignity, without uttering a scream, or a cry, or anything else.

Her body remained there on the kitchen table, with her neck hanging limp and her small eyes staring at death.

The priest was sweeping up when he heard the song. "It's a child," he thought and looked toward the road, but he did not see anyone. Nevertheless, the song was there and it filled the air as if sung by heaven itself.

"You're behind the pine tree," Francisco said in a loud voice.

"No," a voice answered back from the pine tree and just a few seconds later José's head appeared. Francisco thought it was a vision. He was looking at José but José had gone back in time.

"Filuca!" he shouted, confused and immediately he remembered that Filuca couldn't hear, but just the same he called her again. Instead of her, Clarisa appeared.

"Have you gone crazy or what? Why are you calling Filuca when you know she's deaf?"

"So someone will come and tell me if he sees the same thing I see."

"What do you see?"

"That child," he said as he pointed to him.

When Clarisa saw him her heart stopped; shortly after she approached him cautiously so that he would not fly away, so that he would never stop being there. She started to speak to him slowly, trying her best to contain her body's shaking and her desire to cry.

"Salustio!" she shouted suddenly and the priest thought that she had lost her mind when he saw her with that look in her eyes. "We've gone back to the past, Salustio. José is here. Behind the priest's pine tree."

The child understood nothing that was happening and he threw his arms around the trunk of the tree.

That is how he remained until he saw a man approach who looked more or less old to him yet at the same time very agile for his age. He came running with his arms opened wide. The man released him from the tree and held him tightly while he kissed him on the head, the hands, the face, the neck and then murmured:

"My child, my child, thank God. José has come back." Clarisa, kneeling on the ground, kissed his knees and shoes and tried to caress his head.

The child, frightened by the commotion provoked by his presence, attempted to slip away but he could not.

"Let go of him so he can speak to us," said Francisco.

Vitoco, who came out to see what was happening and what all the shouting was about, went back into his house to tell Endina and the children.

At a given moment and with everyone in the village watching what was going on, the child succeeded in freeing himself from the embrace and caresses of the adults.

He was disheveled and his face was filled with terror.

"You must be my grandfather," he said, looking at Salustio.

"You're…You're just the way my father described you. A little bent over and thin. You have eyes that sparkle. You're always about to smile but you never do. Your name is Salustio. Your son's name is José. I'm Jose's son, but don't ask me any questions because I don't remember anything."

Clarisa began to cry and started to overwhelm him with questions.

"Where is José? What's your name? How did you get here? Why didn't he come with you? Did you bring a letter from him? What's your mother's name? Where is your mother? Where have you been all these years?"

"My father was taken away one night. My mother too. That's what I was told. I don't remember anything. I was only a year old, that's all. Little by little I got here. Traveling on the roads, I suppose."

There were no more questions.

The child's name was Gilberto.

That night Salustio could not sleep. He wanted to lose his mind, no matter what, have that crazy look on his face, keep wandering without understanding things and stop thinking right now. He felt as if time was not passing at all, and when he could no longer stand his uneasiness he got dressed and went to the priest's house.

Francisco was eating *digueñes* in his doorway.

"I was expecting you," he said to him.

"What should I do, father?"

"Nothing."

"I never harbored hatred but it has invaded my whole being and now it's killing me. I want to ask you a question. Does God exist?"

"Sometimes."

❁❁❁

Baudilio arrived the next day. It was raining. He went straight to the priest's house and knocked on the door. Francisco looked at him for a minute and then asked:

"What's your name?"

"Baudilio Francisco. And yours?"

"Francisco Baudilio," the priest answered and the two men burst out laughing, then they embraced and that is how they remained without saying another word.

At that same time Salustio and Clarisa had finished the ritual of putting Gilberto to bed. Salustio kissed his head, Clarisa undressed him to wash his body, Salustio took it upon himself to apply ground *quillay* to his hair, she turned him over, Salustio poured the first bucket of warm water on him that Clarisa had perfumed with boldo leaves. Between the two of them they dried him saying words that the child did not understand and among these there was always a "thank you Father for bringing him to us." Then they put on one of the three pajamas that Clarisa had bought for him in Sauzal. She combed his hair, Salustio poured drops of eucalyptus water on his pajama…So that Gilberto would smell the wonderful aroma.

After kissing him and blessing him twice, each one of them, and after Clarisa made the sign of the cross on his forehead, they put him to bed. They covered him and continued to kiss and bless him. Then, they put out the candle and withdrew on tiptoe.

"Tell me the truth, Salustio, do you think Francisco is crazy or not?" Clarisa asked when they were in bed.

"He is one of the holy messengers that God sends to earth," he answered. Then he explained to her that crazy people are something else entirely and that they never foretell events.

"On the contrary, you've got to foretell their future."

He told her that Francisco was not a trickster either.

"Tricksters don't have blue eyes. Theirs are brown with specks of black," he said. As far as the way he says Mass is concerned, he explained that it didn't matter whether you ate a fistful of *maqui* or a cabbage leaf instead of a host. Those have been issues for the Popes down through history, he said, and he told her that the current Pope is number 1,000.

"I'm sure he was the one who ordered that Mass be said backwards or according to the particular taste of each priest. We just don't know, Clarisa. Popes don't come to these small villages that are so far from everything and the song of the distant root is just another song among many."

"No Pope has stated that we are obliged to sing the *Alabado*. Besides, the name distant root is pretty. Wouldn't you like to have a name like that?"

"Do you believe that Francisco obeys the Pope's commands?"

"He does what God asks him to do," Salustio said and his face became translucent.

Clarisa was frightened. "Maybe he's right," she thought.

"Have you been speaking to the *queltehues*?" she asked.

"Yes," he answered, and she thought she saw his face become transparent.

"Tomorrow, early I'll go to his house and I'll ask for forgiveness, and I'll confess my sins and take communion with *maqui*, I'll sing the song of the distant root and I'll ask him to help us find José," Clarisa said and then she fell asleep.

She dreamed that Francisco was flying over the tops of the pine trees singing something that she didn't understand. And crying.

When Clarisa entered the priest's kitchen she found herself

in the presence of two men who were drinking *mate* and speaking secretively. They were sitting by the stove and were so engaged in their conversation that they did not see her.

She held her breath and after observing them for quite a while she ran almost flying out the door, with her arms in the air, asking for help without actually asking, on the verge of screaming and so upset that Salustio became frightened when he saw her coming .

"You were right…He is a saint…A real saint," she mumbled. Salustio didn't understand.

"I'm telling you he is a saint. Now he has multiplied. He performs miracles. Now he's twice the same person and the two of them are drinking *mate* and telling each other secrets."

Salustio still did not understand, but he told her that those are the things that happen to saints. Then he left the house and went to see if what she said was true.

"He didn't split into two. It's his twin brother."

Clarisa became disillusioned.

They spoke no more about it.

❂❂❂

On the following day, after the sun came up, an ox arrived drawing a wagon. It was not Fulgencio, even though it looked like him. He walked with his head held high looking from one side to the other.

Gilberto woke up just then and tiptoed out of the house. He ran to the wagon and just as he was about to climb on board, he stopped. The wagon was not empty. There was a man lying there all curled up. He was dead, but Gilberto did not know how to recognize the dead. "He's sleeping," he thought, and he held on to the wagon with one hand as he walked alongside it. He whistled and from time to time he stood on tiptoe to see if the man continued to sleep.

His face was covered by the collar of his jacket.

When they arrived at Salustio's house, the ox came to a stop and Gilberto ran in.

"Another ox has arrived pulling a wagon. There's a man sleeping inside," he said.

Salustio and Clarisa came out wrapped in their ponchos. Salustio climbed into the wagon and removed the jacket's collar from the sleeping man's face…Suddenly time stopped and his breathing, the blinking of his eyes and his pulse, the tops of the pines and the wind, and a bird that was flying overhead, all were held suspended, and the colors became white and black and everything was left motionless, colorless, without life. And then, in the midst of the silence, Salustio remembered a day in the past, there in the room of their house in the mountains where they lived those first years, and he saw himself opposite Clarisa's bed, who looked at him with sparkling eyes and said:

"Don't look at me like that. I'm not the first woman who's having a baby. He's about to come out. His name is José. Help me and stop looking at me as if I were a ghost."

"If it's a girl her name will be Josefa," he said.

"That's a chicken's name," Clarisa answered and then said it was all right.

A certain time passed and Clarisa's face changed expression.

"Hand me the knife. It's out. It's a boy."

"The knife?" Salustio asked, terrified. What are you going to do with the knife? Where's my child? Have you lost your mind. Say something," he shouted.

Clarisa burst out laughing.

"Hurry up, do it. The baby is between the sheets. Cleaning himself."

Salustio could barely contain his shaking and he handed her the knife.

"I'd better go outside to the patio. My vision is getting blurred," he said and left the room. Outside he found Enedina who had just arrived.

"It's a boy. His name is José. I haven't seen him yet but he's my son," he babbled and went back inside the house.

Now he could not remember what the newborn looked like that Clarisa lifted for him to see. He remembered her sparkling eyes and the face of Enedina who got there late. He remembered that a wave of emotion had taken over his body and that the newborn's cry had penetrated even the most remote corners of his soul, shaking him and leaving him mute and almost without the ability to continue living that moment.

He now thought that it had all been a dream. The birth of his child, the mountains, Tapihue, Francisco, the arrival of the wagon. He thought that he had been dead forever, simply dreaming of life and nothing else.

He looked at the body. Squinted. And the pain invaded him. Clarisa could not take her eyes off him. Tears welled up and anguish enveloped her. Eventually her eyes dried and she suddenly recalled her life with him. Something similar to a frost began to cover her lips. A sadness began to devour her and an endless pain penetrated even the marrow of her bones. She wanted to go away with him, she wanted everything to become dark, for night to be eternal or to be inside him, pressed and hidden inside his throat, invisible and asleep, without having to understand anything, to be without that terrible pain. To be dead.

Salustio and Francisco lowered him from the wagon. Clarisa undressed him, washed his body and dressed him in silence.

On the following day they buried him. Baudilio helped to dig the grave. When the grave was finally covered, the people of Tapihue waited in silence for Francisco's words.

The priest knelt down, for a while he said nothing and then began to speak to the earth. The others began to withdraw slowly.

Salustio and Clarisa remained until the end. The three returned home together. More silent than the dead.

❂❂❂

A few months later Ruth Chandía arrived. Clarisa, who was planting a laurel tree in the front patio of the house, saw her coming. She first thought that it was a vision. Ruth walked with her hips swaying as she tripped over rocks. Her heels were high and pointed. They were not made to be worn on that road. She had a head of black, curly, disheveled hair.

When she saw Clarisa she laughed spontaneously and quickened her pace. Her eyelids were painted blue, her eyelashes covered with black dye, her mouth a fleshy red color and she wore a diamond star pinned to the bodice of her dress.

"What's your name," Clarisa asked, a little annoyed.

"Ruth Chandía. And yours? I'm a friend of Baudilio. Have you seen Baudilio? Why this village doesn't even have a *plaza*. Do you know San Ramón? That's a real town! Shoe stores, barber shops, stores that have everything you could want, bars, restaurants, marvellous dresses in the shop windows. This one I bought there. You like it? It was a little big on me here, look. I like the bust to show a little. Like this, see? Norma did a great job on it, see? But tell me *señora* where does that bandit live?"

"What bandit?"

"Baudilio, who do you think…Maybe I'm in the wrong village. Tell me: is this Tapihue?"

"This is Tapihue, and there's no *plaza* nor stores with everything in them, but there is a church and we do have a priest. There are no bars because the men of Tapihue don't drink."

"Don't get mad, It was just a joke, lady, that's all…"

"My name is Clarisa. Baudilio lives in the house with the blue door," she said and then murmured "don't call me lady," but Ruth did not hear her.

"Baudilio!" Ruth shouted as she knocked on Francisco's door.

The people in the village heard the shouting and stepped outside.

Francisco opened the door and Ruth threw herself on him suffocating him with her enthusiastic embrace while she kissed him on the mouth.

The priest made futile attempts to free himself but Ruth seemed determined to prolong her embrace forever.

When Ruth loosened her hold the priest succeeded in freeing himself. She looked at him the way one looks at a ghost and screamed:

"What's with that cassock? Don't go playing jokes on me! No, not that, no way. A priest, not on your life…"

While all this was going on Baudilio came out of the house and Ruth, without thinking, repeated the same scene all over again. She threw herself at him, gave him a big hug just like the one she gave Francisco, kissed him on the mouth, on his neck and finally she released him.

"You really frightened me. That one's your twin brother, right?"

"How did you find me?" Baudilio asked.

"Did you think you were going to get rid of me that easily? No. Here I am…My love," she said after a bit, as if she were testing the waters.

That night Clarisa told Salustio that she did not like Ruth Chandía.

"She smells like wilted flowers. Her face is all painted up. Her breasts are half way out of her dress. She's one of those bad women, Salustio."

"When did you ever see a bad woman?"

"Never, but I've dreamed about them and that's what they're like. They're like her."

"That's Baudilio's business."

"Baudilio's? Don't play the dummy again, Salustio. Let's be clear: in the priest's house the priest is living with a mute and his brother with a prostitute."

"How do you know?"

"Have you looked in his eyes?"

"No."

"Then look."

Ruth Chandia stayed on in Tapihue. She spent the days dedicated to a variety of tasks that she would repeat at the same time everyday, with the same serenity and devotion.

At eleven o'clock in the morning she got out of bed after eating the breakfast that Filuca served her. She went outside, raised up her arms and greeted the sun: it was to ask the sun to warm her, just like now, for the rest of her days. Then she set up a table and chair next to the door. She sat in the chair and arranged on the table, always in the same way, a group of jars all filled with different kinds of ointment. She then took close to an hour to put her makeup on, and prepare her long silvery nails that Clarisa looked at out of the corner of her eye, making the sign of the cross and murmuring: "Another one of those possessed women."

Baudilio liked Ruth's daily routine and he watched her as if hypnotized while she painted her eyelids blue, her eyebrows green, put rouge on her cheeks and a clear yellow color on the tip of her nose and on the lower part of her jaws.

"Now the lips, Ruth, the lips," Baudilio would say to her and Ruth would select another jar of cream the color of myrtle berries and paint her lips.

"Put more on. So that they shine." And she would put more on.

Around two o'clock Ruth put her jars away in a cardboard box and Baudilio helped her take the table and chair inside. Later they went outside and headed toward the pine trees, laughing as they walked along, she almost losing her balance because of the high heels she was wearing, he with his arm around her waist.

They lay down beneath the pines, kissing and fondling each other, rolling around on the ground; he raising her dress to touch her, she running her nails across his body.

One morning when people in the village saw her take off her black panties Clarisa ran to Francisco's house.

"This can't go on. The children watch what's going on with their eyes popping out of their heads. You've got to do something."

On the following day Baudilio and Ruth Chandía left the village.

That was the day of the birds.

During the night flocks of *queltehues* arrived, speaking all at the same time, excited, taking the words from one another's beak. They were all stirred up and nervous. All of them said the same thing, but the townspeople could not make it out. And immediately after saying what they had to say, all of a sudden they fell to the ground, dead.

More than forty birds were left lying in the street of Tapihue with their wings extended, their necks twisted and their eyes calm.

Neighbors picked them up and buried them near the pine trees. Then they returned to their homes in silence.

❁❁❁

In the middle of that night Enedina woke up. She had not spoken for months.

"Strange things are happening, Vitoco. Strange things have been happening for a long time. The *queltehues* dropped dead without anyone throwing a stone at them. All of them together. As if the devil had something to do with it. The devil and death are stalking this place. I can feel them. I feel them right here," she said as she touched her heart. "Right here."

At that moment she became silent. Soon after she raised her head and said:

"I'm going to kill the children."

Vitoco thought that she had gone crazy again and he got dressed quickly and went to tell Salustio.

"She's sick again!" he shouted when he entered Salustio's house.

"Who?" Salustio asked half awake.

"Enedina. She's got that craziness again."

"The one with the number five?"

"No, it's a different one this time. She says that strange things are happening. And that she's going to kill the children."

"We have to tell Francisco."

The two men left the house. On his way Salustio adjusted his trousers.

The priest also dressed rapidly and the three left for Enedina's house.

They found her sitting in bed with the children scattered on the floor. Their green eyes were wide open, staring at the ceiling.

Francisco knelt down next to each one and took their pulse.

"They're dead, you said you were going to kill them and they overheard you," he said, looking at Enedina. Then he crossed their hands and named each one, one by one, just like the day of their baptism: "Martín, Raúl, Florín, Bernardo, Jesús and Primitivo, in the name of the Son and of the Father, you have always rested in peace but now you are going to rest even more, and you will have the time, all of the time, that only oblivion can bestow."

When the priest and Salustio left the house Vitoco gave his wife a strange look.

"You killed them," he said.

"I was going to kill them, but when I was about to I discovered that they were already dead."

"Children don't end up killing themselves," said Vitoco.

"They never existed," she murmured.

"What are you talking about, Enedina?"

"We invented them."

"But they grew. I saw them. Clarisa saw them, Salustio did too. The priest baptized them."

"In that case they existed," she said and fell off to sleep.

On the following day the priest arrived early at Enedina's house. She continued to sleep while Vitoco attempted to close the children's eyes.

"They'll close later on, in the field where the bright stars shine," said the priest.

"But we can't bury them with their eyes opened," Vitoco replied.

"It doesn't matter," said the priest.

"It does matter. The earth will hurt their eyes."

"The earth can't hurt you," the priest said.

Vitoco kept looking at him and later asked if they could be buried beneath the pines.

When Salustio and Vitoco finished digging, Francisco began to sing the song of the distant root and as he sang the bodies were lowered into the grave. Afterwards they covered them with earth and remained silent listening to the murmur of the pines.

"Are you going to say prayers for the dead?" Clarisa asked.

"Not this time," replied the priest.

They departed in silence and were not aware that it had begun to rain.

On that same day Vitoco and Enedina left the village saying that they were headed for a mountain that nobody knew.

That night Clarisa told Salustio that she wanted to go back to the mountain.

"And what about Gilberto? It's better for him to grow up in a village."

"This isn't a village. It's nothing more than a tomb. We're dying here little by little. Don't you realize this, Salustio? I want to go back. The mountains instill you with sadness but no more than the sadness that already fills us."

"When it stops raining we'll leave," he said.

Before departing Salustio spoke with Francisco.

"I don't want to leave. It's her," he said.

"I know."

"I don't know if I'll be able to live without you, father."

"When you need me, call me. I'm not moving from this place."

❂❂❂

A week later three men arrived. They entered the priest's house and when they saw Filuca they began asking her questions.

"She's deaf and dumb," said Francisco.

"You think we're going to believe you?"

"I don't think anything," the priest said.

One of the men approached him and struck him in the face; then he took some stakes from his knapsack, drove them into the ground and tied the priest's ankles to the stakes.

Between the three of them they carried her off. Filuca tried to defend herself but she couldn't. She turned her head twice and looked at the priest with a sad look in her eyes. Francisco also looked at her.

When he lost sight of them as they turned a bend in the road, he lowered his head and began to cry.

The years went by. Time dragged slowly on and Francisco lived suspended without knowing that hours, days, weeks, and months were coming and going. He slept little. In the morning he sang the song of the distant root. In the afternoon he looked at the sky and cried. Sometimes he sketched Filuca's eyes on a piece of paper and stared at them. Later he would tell her secrets and fall asleep with the piece of paper in his hand.

✪✪✪

Gilberto was playing in the patio when his grandfather called him. The child entered the room and saw Clarisa in bed.

"I want you to go to Tapihue and look for a thin man. He has the face of a saint. When you find him tell him to come. Tell him that Clarisa is lying in bed with her eyes opened, and tell him that I need him. You have to speak loud to him because he's an old man. Then give him the hen. Tell him that your grandfather sent it."

"I can't. They say that he has a pact with the devil. They say he's not a man and that he came into the world as an old man. He frightens me," Gilberto said.

"The devil doesn't exist and the father is a man just like me. Don't you remember when you were a child he used to take you in his arms and sit you on his shoulders. He was the first one to see you when you arrived in Tapihue." Salustio stood in the doorway until he could no longer make him out. Then he went back into the house and sat beside the bed. She seemed to be asleep.

Clarisa smiled at him with her eyes closed.

"I'm dead, Salustio," she said to him but he did not hear her. He drew near, almost up against her ear, and slowly, so as not to wake her up, he told her that Gilberto had gone to Tapihue to get the priest.

"I sent him the hen and if he comes we'll give him the pig. He's old but he'll come. I know him."

Clarisa smiled again.

Salustio thought that as soon as Francisco arrived he would wake her up. "She's tired," he thought.

"You're just tired," he said to her, but she scarcely heard his voice. She was already far from that room.

"I'm going to get José," she yelled to him from the doorway and then set off on a different road. She wore a white nightdress and carried a bunch of laurel in her hand. Tall and thin, with black hair and the smell of the *quillay* tree about her. She walked almost on tiptoe, looking from side to side. It was a solitary field without beginning or end. In the distance several stars hung like bright oranges, but they were much farther away than they appeared and it was impossible to touch them. Suddenly she saw an old man sitting on a mound of earth. He held a rosary in his hands. He was talking to the earth. She approached him and the man raised his head.

"Where's José?" she said to him.

"I haven't seen him," he replied; then he lowered his head and continued speaking to himself.

"Where can I find him?" Clarisa interrupted.

"There's no end to this," he said.

"You must have seen him go by," Clarisa insisted.

"No," he replied.

There was no way of getting any more information from him. Clarisa remained for a while just looking at him and trying to understand his words. Then she left him and kept walking. Further on she came to a stop. She sensed that there was no noise, no air, nothing.

"José!" she shouted, but her shout dissolved. She walked a little bit more and when she sensed that the silence was becoming more and more intense, she decided to return home. Salustio was where she left him. He was looking at her with his face turned to one side.

"I'm another person. I can come and go even though my body is physically lying in this bed. I already departed once. There was an old man, stars that looked like blue oranges and a great silence. I still haven't seen José, but death is infinite. I have all the time in the world to find him," Clarisa said. Salustio was not listening.

Nor was he aware that she stood in front of the mirror and looked at herself.

The thin nightdress showed the outline of her bones. Everything about her seemed to be from some other place. The extreme whiteness of her face, her hands that seemed to be made of air from her finger nails on down, and her smile like that of an angel painted on the wall of a church.

"I look beautiful," Clarisa said and she began to move around the room. She went from side to side, almost flying, as if she were made of smoke. Suddenly, she approached Salustio and caressed his face.

Next she opened the closet, put on José's coat and started to sing the song of the distant root. Outside there were birds. They listened to her. A cold wind blew through the branches of the pine trees.

She spent a good deal of time like that, singing and moving as if she were water, without either sorrow or happiness entering her and without worrying about the fact that time was elapsing.

At midnight Gilberto returned from Tapihue.

"I gave him the hen," he said.

"Did you tell him that I needed him?" Salustio asked.

"I told him. And he replied that he was on his way. He said for you to wait for him and not fall asleep. I'm old and I walk slowly. That's what he said."

"Did you tell him that your grandmother is lying in bed with her eyes shut?"

The boy didn't answer.

"Did you tell him that Clarisa is lying in bed with her eyes shut?" Salustio insisted.

Gilberto remained silent and then left the room.

✿✿✿

Francisco's bones ached when he bent over to tie his shoe laces. "Salustio's house is a long way from here," he thought. "Everything is far away…Even the first days in Tapihue and the hurricane of evil beasts that left this land so dark, and the men who weren't men and the women traveling the roads with that lost look on their faces, and the hidden children. Fear entered through the cracks and it took control of everyone, even the animals, the pine trees and the stream."

The years, the months and the days had become jumbled for Francisco, and if those times were so clear in his memory it was because he could not forget Filuca's eyes when the men took her away. For years he dreamed the same dream: Filuca looked at him and he remained frozen in place. Filuca tried to speak to him but he could not understand her. Then he tried to guess at what she was saying by looking into her eyes, but her eyes were made of black water and bereft of a gaze. At that moment he understood that they were going to kill her and he freed himself from the stakes and attacked the men, but when he was almost on top of them, Filuca and the men disappeared. Francisco looked for them everywhere but he could find no one.

Now Salustio was calling for him. "It will take me four days," he thought. He popped a handful of *digueñes* in his mouth and headed toward the mountains.

Salustio touched Clarisa's forehead. It was cold but he was not aware of this. "My hands are warm from rubbing them so much. Maybe I'm getting a fever," he thought, and he believed that he might die.

"I'm not going to die, Clarisa, don't worry," he said to her and then he took her hand.

"Don't pretend you don't realize what's going on, Salustio. I know you know that I'm dead. You'll never change. Say something to me for the dead. Don't keep looking at me like that!" she said to him almost shouting; then she tried to look more dead than she really was, as dead as she could possibly look, but she could not. Her body was rigid, her face white, her lips taut, her jaws tight, her bones cold and a smell of withered roses began to fill the room.

"Josefa wasn't just any old hen, Clarisa. When you wake up I'm going to explain," Salustio said.

"Yes, I know you will," she answered.

"I never told you that when you killed her I went and hid behind the myrtle bushes. I felt like crying. When you wake up I'll tell you."

"I know you will," Clarisa repeated.

"It was because I loved her, but I have to explain it all to you. When you wake up." She answered him from the doorway.

"I'm going back to the field. To see if I can find José."

The old man was sitting on the same mound of earth with the rosary in his hands, his head lowered more than before, as if giving kisses to the ground.

"Have you seen José," Clarisa asked again.

The old man remained exactly as before.

"Have you seen him?" she insisted.

The old man raised his head a little. He looked at her askance just like the first time, and he told her he did not want to answer her questions.

"Leave me alone. I don't want to be bothered," he said.

Clarisa withdrew from that place and, just like before, she entered the silent field. The light seemed different this time, the stars had moved farther away. She was looking at them when she noticed a young woman walking in her direction and when they were face to face they looked at each other.

"You still can't speak?" Clarisa asked her.

"No, now I can," Filuca said and she began to sing the song of the distant root. Afterwards she remained silent and then spoke in a slow, hoarse voice.

"Those of us who have been murdered we can't come and go like you."

"They tear away our life in chunks and we reach the field feeling the terror of the final night. I would love to but I can't go to Francisco and tell him about the last night of my life. I would also like to caress his head and kiss his hands and ask him to listen to me..." Filuca started to sing the song of the distant root and then she looked at Clarisa.

"If you see him," she added, "take him this bracelet. Tell him it's Filuca's bracelet and then tell him that you saw me. Tell him I know how to sing the song of the distant root."

"If you see José tell him that I'm looking for him," Clarisa said and she headed back to where she came from, with the bracelet in her hand.

When she entered the house she saw that Salustio had not moved from her side.

"Filuca speaks and listens, just like us. She gave me this silver bracelet. She wants me to give it to the priest," she said. Salustio did not hear her but he saw the bracelet in her hand.

"Clarisa!" he shouted and shook her by the shoulders. "Wake up, Clarisa!" he kept shouting. "Where did you get that bracelet? You didn't have it a while ago. My God! Wake up, Clarisa, once and for all."

At that moment the bracelet fell to the floor and Clarisa's hand was left dangling.

Salustio's breathing was suddenly interrupted and a wave of anguish obstructed his throat. He touched her forehead, he opened her eyes, then he attempted to sit her up in bed, next he tried to separate her fingers and finally he remained looking at her with great sorrow.

Clarisa did not wish to see him like that. A grief for the dead ran through her bones.

Three days went by. She never moved from where she was,

but shortly before the priest's arrival she decided to go to the field. "So they'll be able to talk in peace," she thought and then she left.

❁❁❁

When Francisco entered the house the silence weighed like a sleeping ox. Everything seemed to be moving even though all was quiet. One could hear the walls breathing and the air was thick.

The priest arrived and waited a moment in the doorway. Salustio did not hear him. He continued sitting beside Clarisa's body, looking at her intensely as if he had never seen her before.

Francisco did not move. He took out a handful of *digueñes* and popped them in his mouth.

Salustio heard a noise and turned his head. He confronted those blue eyes and tried to say something, but the priest did not let him.

"It's not necessary," he said. "Don't look at her like that. Clarisa doesn't like it."

"She's dead," Salustio uttered.

"She was about to return to the field," the priest said.

"She's dead! And you're crazy. She's never going to return. The dead don't return. They go away forever, father, forever. Look at her face!"

"And the bracelet?"

"What bracelet?"

"Filuca's bracelet. Where did you leave it?"

Salustio started to shake. His eyes grew bigger. He looked at the priest as if he were looking at a ghost. He could not say anything nor could he stop looking into the infinite eyes that were looking back at him serenely and calmly.

"Death is an invention," said the priest.

"Salustio started to tremble."

"And what about the bodies of the dead? And the worms? And the staring eyes? And that smell that's in this room? And Clarisa's cold hands? And José's body tossed into the wagon? And the gasp that suddenly escapes? And the flesh that rots and separates from the bones? And what about Clarisa dead, right here, and the two of us looking at her? All of this is an invention?" he asked, and then continued shouting: The devil's priest. Clarisa was right. Trickster, a priest that lies. Death is an invention, you say, and you look at me with the same look the devil gave you before he sent you. And this dead woman was my wife? What is she? A cold and stiff invention in a bed? And my son who was born beneath these sheets and later returned stiff in a wagon, with his face very white, his eyes open forever and without being able to speak? What was that? Another invention? Answer me! Say that the devil sent you. Say it, father, or I'll kill you."

Francisco said nothing.

"And what about the bracelet?" he asked after a while.

"Where is the bracelet?"

"What bracelet?"

"Filuca's bracelet. Where did you leave it?"

Salustio shook again, then lowered his head and fell asleep. Francisco let him be. He sat on a stool and there he remained waiting. Ten minutes went by and Salustio woke up. His face had changed. There was no anger now in his eyes. He looked at the priest and then picked up Filuca's bracelet that had been left on the floor.

"Here it is…Clarisa had it in her hands," he said and then he handed it to him.

Francisco raised his head, stretched his bent body, then stood on his tiptoes, raised his arms with his fists clenched and continued to stretch until he touched the ceiling. Then little by little he began to unwind like a cord as if the force of gravity did not exist. He got up from the floor, sat down on the stool next to Clarisa's bed and handed the bracelet to Salustio. He said nothing, but since Salustio thought he heard "do the same thing", he got up, stretched his body and continued to extend it until he reached the ceiling. Next he unwound just as the priest had done and kept falling until he rolled up into a ball on the floor. Then he stood up and sat on the stool at the other side of Clarisa's bed.

They did the same thing several times. In silence…Until they became tired and stayed seated, one opposite the other, looking at each other.

❂❂❂

A short time before nightfall Gilberto entered the room. The bed was made and alongside it were two stools.

"They left," said the boy and he shut the door.

JUNE 1988

GLOSSARY

Alabado: a hymn sung or recited in honor of the Eucharist.

Calladito: a dance popular in the rural, agricultural areas of Chile in which three people dance together.

Cazuela: a popular dish in Chile made of meat or chicken, corn, and vegetables and seasoned with red pepper.

Chanchos en piedra: a kind of puree made of onions, garlic, corian der and tomatos.

Corrido: a popular ballad patterned after the Spanish "romance" of the eighteenth century.

Diguenes: a parasitic fungus that grows on certain types of oak trees. In the majority of cases they are edible, round, round in shape, sweet to the taste and found in central and southern Chile.

Mate: a tea-like beverage made from the leaves of the mate tree.

Mote: stewed corn.

Queltehue: a bird common to Chile whose habitat extends all the way from the Atacama region of Chile. It lives in irrigated fields and pastures and is known for its strong, strident cry. Long legged, it has a gray neck and head, red pointed beak, green colored wings with shades of black and white and a white tail with shades of black.

Qillayes: a soapbark tree.

Quintrales: the generic name for several types of parasitic bushes of the Lorantacheae family that produce flowers of brilliant color. It is common to cut away these bushes since they undermine the health of the trees to which they adhere.